WITH JESUS
I Don't Give Up

Copyrights

www.gnmkids.com

This book belongs to:

....

....

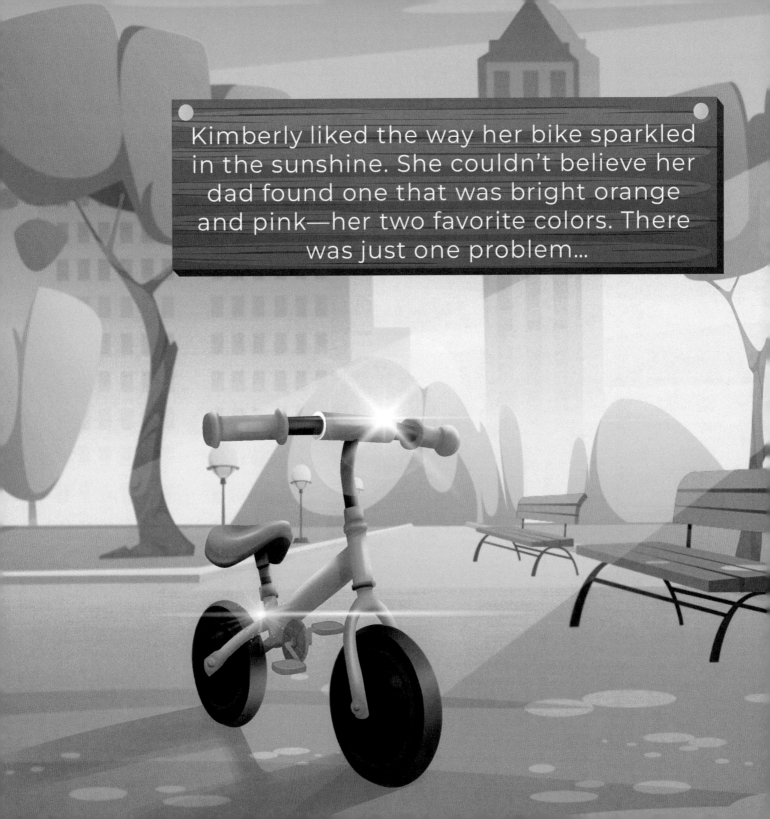

Kimberly liked the way her bike sparkled in the sunshine. She couldn't believe her dad found one that was bright orange and pink—her two favorite colors. There was just one problem...

Kimberly couldn't ride it. She had tried really hard, but no matter how hard she tried she couldn't keep her bike from falling over.

"Don't give up! You'll get the hang of it," her dad said. "Once you learn, you'll see how much fun it is," her mom said. "It's easy. You just have to balance," her brother said.

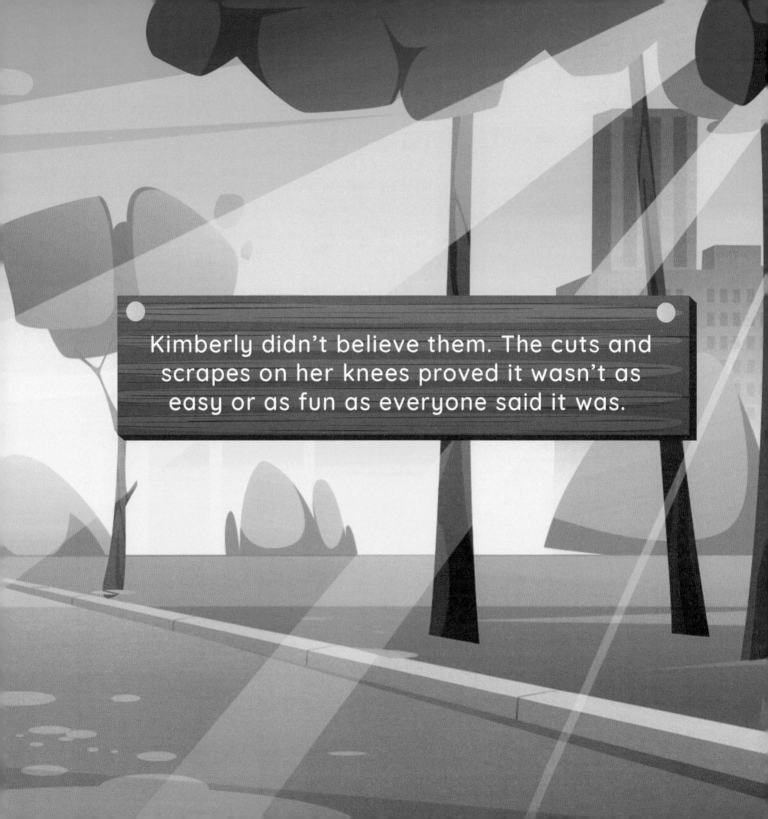

Kimberly didn't believe them. The cuts and scrapes on her knees proved it wasn't as easy or as fun as everyone said it was.

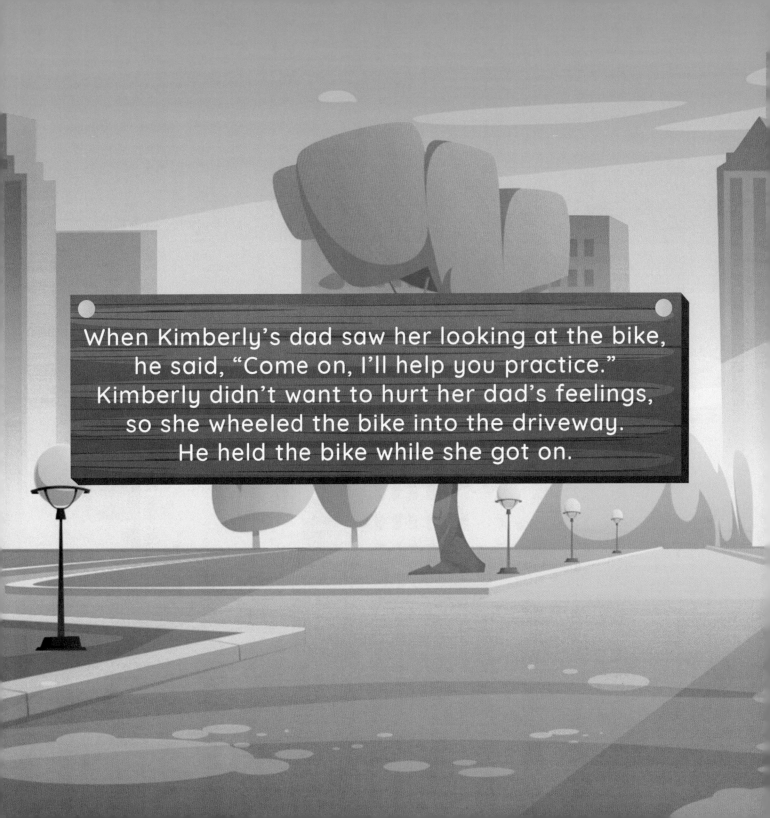

When Kimberly's dad saw her looking at the bike, he said, "Come on, I'll help you practice." Kimberly didn't want to hurt her dad's feelings, so she wheeled the bike into the driveway. He held the bike while she got on.

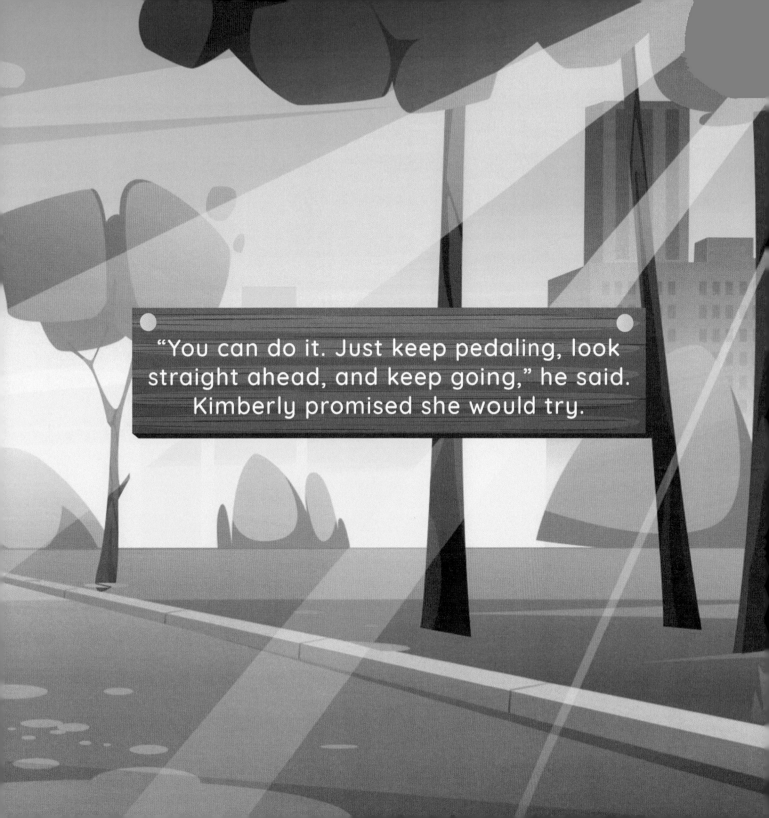

"You can do it. Just keep pedaling, look straight ahead, and keep going," he said. Kimberly promised she would try.

Dad gave her a little push to get started. She made it to the next driveway and then... down she went. "I give up! I can't do this!" she cried.

"I'm sorry, Dad, but I am never going to be able to do this." "Kimberly," her dad said, "do you remember the lesson you had in Sunday School last week?" "The one about Peter catching all those fish?" she asked.

"Yes," her dad said. "Sure. Peter fished all night without catching anything. The next morning Jesus told him to put the fishing net into the water again, and when he did, Peter caught more fish than he could count.""That's right," Dad smiled. "Peter trusted Jesus instead of..."

"Instead of giving up," Kimberly finished her dad's sentence. Dad nodded. "Do you think I'll be able to ride my bike if I trust Jesus like Peter did?" Kimberly asked.

"I sure do," Dad said. "Jesus," Kimberly prayed, "I know that you are with me, and I'll try again.
Thank you, Jesus. Amen."

After her dad helped her get on the bike, Kimberly started pedaling. She said, "I'm not giving up, Jesus. I'm trusting that you won't let me fall." And guess what?

Jesus helped her! Kimberly rode her bike to the end of the block and back! "Thanks, Dad, for reminding me that instead of giving up, we should ask Jesus to help us...and he will!

The End.

And Simon answering said unto him, Master, we have toiled all the night, and have taken nothing: nevertheless at thy word I will let down the net. And when they had this done, they inclosed a great multitude of fishes: and their net brake.

Luke 5v5-6 KJV

Author's note:

Thank you so much for reading this book. If you enjoyed this book, we would love it if you could leave a review and recommend it to a friend.

If there is anything you would like to share with us to help us improve this book, please go to gnmkids.com/feedback

Please checkout our other books

www.gnmkids.com

Made in the USA
Las Vegas, NV
16 November 2024